OUR
St. Patrick's Day
BOOK

by Sandra Ziegler
illustrated by Gwen Connelly

THE
CHILD'S
WORLD

ELGIN, ILLINOIS 60120

Distributed by Childrens Press, 1224 West Van Buren Street, Chicago, Illinois 60607.

Library of Congress Cataloging in Publication Data

Ziegler, Sandra, date
  Our St. Patrick's Day book.

  (A Special-day book)
  Summary: Describes a class's
activities in preparation for St. Patrick's Day.
   1. St. Patrick's Day—Juvenile literature.
2. St. Patrick's Day decorations—Juvenile literature.
[1. St. Patrick's Day]   I. Connelly, Gwen, ill.
II. Title.   III. Series.
GT4995.P3Z54   1987   394.2'6828   86-31726
ISBN 0-89565-344-3

1 2 3 4 5 6 7 8 9 10 11 12 R 96 95 94 93 92 91 90 89 88 87

OUR
St. Patrick's Day
BOOK

This book is about how we celebrated St. Patrick's Day in our class. You will have more ideas in your class.

On St. Patrick's Day, Miss O'Day
put a colorful picture on the bulletin
board. "Top o' the mornin'," she said
when we came to school.

That's an Irish way of saying, "Have
a nice day."

"Top o' the mornin', Miss O'Day,"
we all said.

"I wore my green skirt and my shamrock," said Erin. "My mom said everyone who is Irish should wear green on St. Patrick's Day."

"Who is St. Patrick?" asked Sally.

"St. Patrick was a Catholic missionary who lived in Ireland long ago," said Miss O'Day.

"St. Patrick started churches and schools. He helped the Irish people a lot."

She showed us a picture of St. Patrick ringing his school bell.

"St. Patrick's Day is a holiday in
Ireland. And Irish people in other
lands celebrate too," said Miss O'Day.

"In the United States, many large

cities have parades on St. Patrick's
Day. People wear green shamrocks
and hats. And they wave green flags.
Even the horses wear green. And the
bands play Irish music."

"What's a shamrock?" asked Danny.

"A shamrock is a special plant from Ireland," said Miss O'Day. "It's also the national emblem of Ireland, just as an eagle is the United States emblem. A shamrock is always green."

We all wanted to make shamrocks, so. . .

Miss O'Day let us make shamrock pins.

You can make one too.

Cut three green
hearts.

Cut a green stem.

Glue the leaves
and stem together
to make a shamrock.

Tape a clip be-
hind the shamrock.
Then clip it to your
clothes. Or attach
a small safety
pin behind the
shamrock.

"Now we will play, 'Can You?'" Miss O'Day said. She asked Tom, "Can you put eight shamrocks on the board?"

"I can," Tom said. And he did.

"Next, Miss O'Day asked, "Sally, can you find the numeral that tells how many there are?"

Sally did. She put the numeral eight
by the eight shamrocks.

"Now you may all take turns doing
other numbers," Miss O'Day said. She
let us choose and match whatever
numbers we wanted.

Later, Tom wanted to know who the little green men on the picture were.

"They are leprechauns," Miss O'Day said. "Leprechauns are the fairies of Ireland."

Then Miss O'Day told us about
leprechauns. . .

"A leprechaun is a tricky little man. He is always dressed in green," she said. "He has a pot of gold. He hides it carefully. If you catch a leprechaun, he must give his gold to you."

"How do you catch a leprechaun?" Carlos asked.

"You look for one in the moon-light," Miss O'Day said. "Look under

a leaf. Remember that a leprechaun
is not any bigger than my thumb.

"Listen. You might hear one going,
'Tap-tap; tap-tap.' A leprechaun makes
shoes for fairies—one shoe at a time.
You could catch him working.

"Be careful though. Never let a
leprechaun see you. Just sneak up
and grab him. Don't take your eyes off
him. If you do, he'll trick you. And
he'll quickly disappear."

"I wish I could catch a leprechaun,"
Sally said.

"Maybe you can," said Miss O'Day.
She let us play, "Catch the Leprechaun."
We played it like tag.

First Tom was the leprechaun. He carried a pot of gold.

Betsy caught Tom. He had to give his gold to her. Then Betsy was the leprechaun.

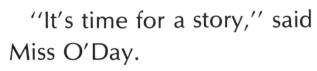

"It's time for a story," said Miss O'Day.

"Tell a leprechaun story," Beth said. So Miss O'Day told us this—

"I caught you, Mr. Leprechaun," Mike said, jumping about. "Now take me to your gold."

"That's the rule," said Mr. Leprechaun. And he showed Mike the way to a field of goldenrods.

22

"My crock of gold is under a plant," said Mr. Leprechaun. "But you will need a shovel to dig it up. My shovel is behind that tree over there." "Which tree?" asked Mike, looking to see.

When Mike looked back, Mr. Leprechaun was gone. Never trust a leprechaun. He'll trick you every time.

"Let's write a story about a leprechaun," said Miss O'Day. "You help me. Let's see if we can use the sound of the letter 'l' in our story."

Here is what we wrote.

"Our leprechaun is called Larry," Beth said.

"He has a pot of gold," Erin said.

"Nobody can catch Larry Leprechaun," said Tom. "He leaps away."

"He likes to hide under a leaf," said Sally.

"I think Larry Leprechaun laughs a lot," Billy said.

Then we all laughed. That was the end of our story.

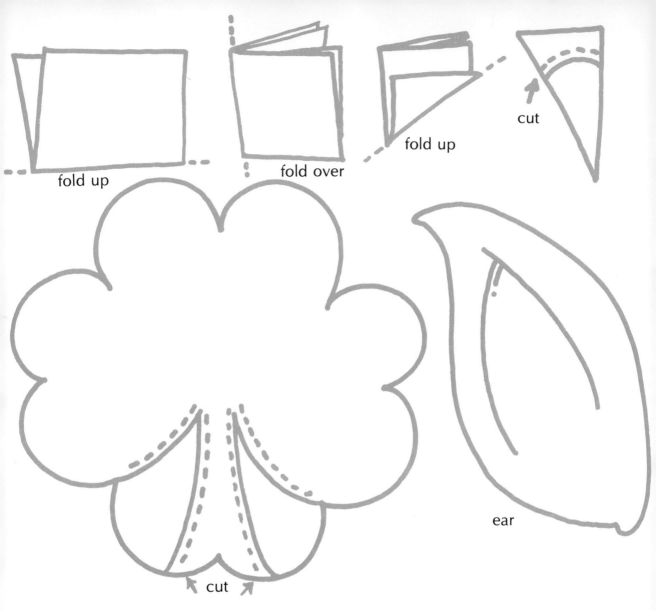

fold up

fold over

fold up

cut

cut

ear

"Now let's make special shamrock leprechauns," said Miss O'Day.

"First Miss O'Day showed us how to cut big shamrocks out of sheets of green paper. Then we made elfin ears, a happy face, and a leprechaun hat. Our leprechauns looked like this.

nose

mouth

ear

eyes

27

"I can be a leprechaun," said Tom.
He held up his leprechaun and did a
funny, leaping, tiptoe dance for us.

Note: A simple jig could be taught to children to transform this song into a dance vehicle.

"Lots of Irish people like to dance," said Miss O'Day. She played an Irish dancing song. She called it a jig. She said we could all dance. So we did.

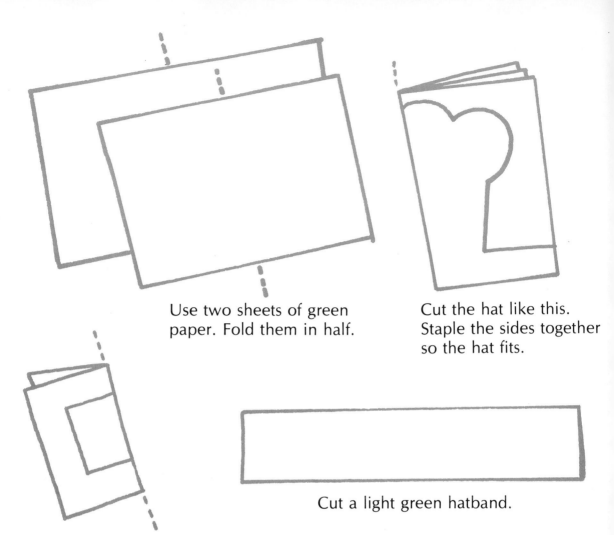

Use two sheets of green paper. Fold them in half.

Cut the hat like this. Staple the sides together so the hat fits.

Cut a yellow buckle.

Cut a light green hatband.

"I could dress up like a leprechaun," Danny said. "I have a green shirt at home."

"Then you would need a hat," said Miss O'Day. She showed us how to make hats.

When it was time to go home,
Danny tipped his hat to Miss O'Day.
''Top o' the afternoon,'' he said.

''Top o' the afternoon, Danny,''
Miss O'Day said. Then she smiled her
Irish smile.